SE 1 '99

Sp̶o̶o̶k̶y̶ ̶S̶p̶

WITHDRAWN

There are more books about the Bailey City Monsters!

Spooky Spells

by **Marcia Thornton Jones**
and
Debbie Dadey

illustrated by **John Steven Gurney**

A
LITTLE APPLE
PAPERBACK

SCHOLASTIC INC.
New York   Toronto   London   Auckland   Sydney
Mexico City   New Delhi   Hong Kong

For my best buddy from Henderson County Senior High, Karen Dodson, and her family. And to the great kids at Gale School in Galesburg, IL, and Jefferson School in Appleton, WI.

— DD

To all those extra-special students and teachers who make magic happen every day!

— MTJ

No part of this publication may be reproduced in whole or in part, or stored in a retrieval system, or transmitted in any form or by any means, electronic, mechanical, photocopying, recording, or otherwise, without written permission of the publisher. For information regarding permission, write to Scholastic Inc., Attention: Permissions Department, 555 Broadway, New York, NY 10012.

ISBN 0-439-05871-6

Text copyright © 1999 by Marcia Thornton Jones and Debra S. Dadey. Illustrations copyright © 1999 by Scholastic Inc. All rights reserved. Published by Scholastic Inc. SCHOLASTIC, LITTLE APPLE PAPERBACKS, THE BAILEY CITY MONSTERS, and associated logos are trademarks and/or registered trademarks of Scholastic Inc.

12 11 10 9 8 7 6 5 4 3 2   9/9 0 1 2 3 4/0

Printed in the U.S.A.   40

First Scholastic printing, April 1999

Contents

1
Spelling Bee

"Just you wait," Issy told Jane on the playground after school. "I'll be the winner of the school spelling bee. I'm the best speller Bailey City has ever seen."

Jane rolled her dark eyes at Issy. "You're not the only good speller around," Jane said. "I happen to know that Annie and Ben are good, too." Jane pointed to her friend Annie, who was swinging on the jungle gym across the playground. Annie's brother, Ben, was in the same fourth-grade class as Issy and Jane.

Issy tossed her straight brown hair back and looked at Ben, who was hanging upside down from the jungle gym. "You'll have to do better than Ben and his little bitty third-grade sister to beat me. I don't even have to study. I happen to have a very high IQ."

1

Jane felt like sticking her tongue out at Issy or throwing dirt on her frilly dress. But Jane didn't. Ben did.

"Hey, Issy," Ben said, sliding up beside Issy, causing dust to fly onto her dress. "How's life in the vacuum cleaner?"

Issy quickly wiped the dust off her dress. "Vacuum cleaner?" she asked.

"That's where you got your brains, wasn't it?" Ben teased. "A vacuum cleaner is full of lots of little tiny dust balls, just like your head."

"Well, I never," Issy said, stomping away from Ben.

Ben stuck his tongue out at Issy. "Well, maybe you should sometime, you might be a little nicer!"

Jane usually didn't like it when Ben was rude, but this time she had to agree. "That Issy makes me so mad sometimes," Jane said. "She acts like the rest of us are stupid. She's not the only one who could win the spelling bee."

"It doesn't bother me," Ben said as

Annie and their friend Kilmer walked up beside him.

"What doesn't bother you?" Annie asked.

"That Issy thinks she's so smart she can beat everyone in spelling without even trying," Jane explained.

"Issy is pretty smart," Kilmer admitted. "She always gets one hundreds on the classroom spelling tests." Kilmer was in fourth grade, too. But Kilmer didn't look like an ordinary fourth-grader. He was at least a head taller than Ben, and his hair was flat on top like a Frankenstein monster. Kilmer had recently moved to Bailey City from Transylvania.

"She makes me so mad with her bragging," Jane said. "I wish I could find a way to beat her in the spelling bee."

"I know a way," Annie told Jane.

2
Magical Bug

"I know how to beat Issy," Annie said as the kids started walking home.

Jane looked both ways before crossing Forest Lane and said, "Well, don't keep us in suspense. Tell us."

"The way to beat Issy at the spelling bee is to study," Annie told her friends.

"Study?" Ben snorted. "If that's the only way to win, then you can count me out." Studying was definitely not Ben's favorite thing to do.

"What kind of bug is this spelling bee, anyway?" Kilmer asked.

Annie, Ben, and Jane stopped at the turnoff to Dedman Street and stared at Kilmer.

"Is it a magical bug that can do incanta-

5

tions?" he asked. "I have never heard of this type of insect."

Ben snickered, but Annie explained spelling bees to Kilmer. "It isn't a bug at all," Annie said. "A spelling bee is a contest."

Jane nodded. "It's a contest to see who can say the correct order of each letter in a word."

Kilmer bopped a hand on the side of his square forehead. "Oh, how silly of me. I was thinking of a wizard's spells and incantations."

"It's an easy mistake," Ben said. "Now, how about we run home and play some softball?"

Annie adjusted her backpack on her shoulder and started to walk up Dedman Street. "I think we should study for the spelling bee," Annie said. "After all, it's tomorrow."

Ben groaned. "Who cares about a spelling bee?"

"The winner gets a gift certificate to Dover's," Jane reminded him.

Ben bent his hand down and swayed his hips. "That's just lovely," he said sarcastically. "I'll win so I can get new hair clips from Dover's."

"Very funny," Annie said. "Dover's sells more than hair clips. Now, who wants to study words with me?"

Jane didn't raise her hand. Ben didn't raise his hand, but Kilmer did. Ben looked at Kilmer as if he had broccoli for brains. "Are you crazy?" Ben asked. "It's a beautiful day. Let's play ball."

"I think it might be fun to do this spelling bee," Kilmer said. "I have never tried it before."

Ben glared at Annie. "Thanks a lot," Ben said. "Now I have no one to play with."

"What do I look like?" Jane asked. "Chopped liver?"

Ben didn't answer Jane. Instead, he stopped dead in his tracks and pointed straight at Hauntly Manor Inn.

3

On Wheels

"What is it?" Annie asked.

"It looks like a haunted house on wheels," Ben said.

Jane nodded and stared at the huge mobile home. It had spiderwebs hanging off the broken shutters and all the windows were cracked. A tall, thin man with long white hair and a beard stood outside the home. He wore a long flowing robe and a pointed cap on his head.

"That man must be at least a hundred years old," Jane said.

"No," Kilmer said, "he's thousands of years old. It's Great-uncle Nilrem!" Kilmer stomped down Dedman Street just as his parents came outside.

"Uncle Nilrem!" Kilmer's mother, Hilda Hauntly, rushed over to hug her uncle.

Kilmer's father practically flew across the brown lawn to greet Uncle Nilrem.

"It looks like a monster reunion," Jane whispered to Annie and Ben. The kids stared at the strange group before them. Hilda wore the same stained lab coat she always wore and her wild hair stood up all over her head. Kilmer's father, Boris, reminded Annie of Count Dracula. Boris wrapped his long black cape around Nilrem and hugged him.

"Great-uncle Nilrem," Kilmer said, "I want you to meet my friends." Kilmer motioned for the kids to come closer. "This is Ben, Annie, and Jane."

Nilrem bowed. "It is my great pleasure to meet friends of my dear nephew Kilmer."

Annie smiled and curtsied. "We're happy to meet you, too."

"That's a cool mobile home you have there," Ben said, nodding toward the unusual house on wheels.

Nilrem bowed again. "It meets my needs."

Hilda took her uncle's hand and told everyone, "We must go inside for refreshments. I just made up a batch of pickled pig's feet."

Annie's face turned green and she quickly said, "We'd love to, but we have to study for the spelling contest. I really want to win this year."

"A spelling contest?" Nilrem asked. "That sounds so interesting. I'm quite a good speller myself. I'm sure I could help you."

Boris patted Nilrem's shoulder. "Uncle Nilrem is a master speller," Boris said to the kids. "He has taught some of the greatest of all time."

Nilrem blushed and bowed once again.

"With my uncle helping you," Hilda said, "no one could beat you in a spelling contest."

4
Has-been

"Wait," Kilmer said before his great-uncle Nilrem could utter a word. "Annie and Jane explained to me that a spelling bee is correctly naming the letters of a word in order."

The smile faded from Nilrem's face. "There's nothing magical about saying letters," he said sadly.

"What did you think a spelling bee was?" Jane asked.

Nilrem's shoulders sagged. "It doesn't matter. What I feared must be true. I am just an old has-been. There's no use for my kind of *spell*ing in this day and age."

"I'm sure you could help us," Annie said.

Nilrem smiled broadly and hugged Kilmer. "It would bring me great joy to help my dear nephew and his friends."

14

Jane pulled Annie and Ben to the side. "We can't let him help us win the spelling bee," Jane whispered. "It wouldn't be fair."

"Why not?" Annie asked quietly. "Anyone can help you practice."

Jane looked at Nilrem's long flowing robe. It was covered with stars, moons, and funny symbols. "There's something very mysterious about him," Jane whispered.

Ben dropped his backpack down by his foot and glared at Jane. "You are so picky. First you say you would do anything to beat old Issy, but when someone offers to help, you won't let them."

Nilrem glided over to Ben, Annie, and Jane. "Is anything wrong?" Nilrem asked.

"Oh, no," Annie said. "We were just saying how nice it was for you to offer to help us."

Jane groaned. "Now something really is wrong," she said.

"What?" Nilrem and Ben asked together.

"Here comes Issy," Jane said.

Issy pranced up beside the kids and

16

stuck her nose up in the air. "I'm going to my dance lessons," she told them.

"I thought you'd be studying for the spelling bee," Annie said.

Issy giggled and put one hand on Annie's shoulder. "I'm really lucky," Issy said. "I can learn things just by glancing at them. It's a talent I have."

Jane felt like saying something rude, but Issy beat her to it. Issy turned to Nilrem's mobile home and squealed, "What is that horrible-looking thing?"

Annie's face turned red. "That's Kilmer's great-uncle Nilrem's house, and it's not horrible!"

"That's right," Jane said. "It's very special."

"Ew-weee!" Issy squealed again. "It's disgusting."

Nilrem stood in front of Issy. "Allow me to present myself. I am Kilmer's great-uncle Nilrem."

Issy put her hands on her hips. "Well, that explains it," Issy said. "Everything to do with Kilmer is weird, weird, WEIRD! I'm getting out of here before any of it rubs off on me."

Issy stomped down the street, but not before Ben shouted, "It's too late. You're the strangest one of all!"

Annie patted Nilrem on the shoulder. "I'm sorry Issy was so rude," she said. "She's like that to everyone."

"That does it!" Jane hollered. "I've had it with that Issy. It's time we get even with her!"

5
Ben's Plan

"I know exactly what we need to do," Ben told Jane as soon as Issy disappeared down Dedman Street.

Jane grinned. "I knew I could count on you," she told Ben. "What's your plan?"

Ben leaned close to Jane so he could whisper in her ear. Annie stepped near them so she could hear, too, but she could have been standing at the end of Dedman Street because Ben didn't whisper. He yelled, "PLAY BALL!"

Jane covered her ears, Annie jumped, and Kilmer ducked. But Nilrem smiled so big his eyes disappeared in wrinkles. "Your words have power enough to stir the clouds!"

"Even your uncle agrees," Ben said.

"Issy's ruined enough of our afternoon. Let's forget about Issy and play ball."

"Of course I agree," Nilrem told them. "My ball is right inside my home." He turned to swing open the narrow door to the black motor home. Nilrem's robe swirled about him as he disappeared inside. Ben, Annie, and Jane moved closer, hoping to see inside, but Nilrem reappeared so fast that the kids jumped back three steps, only catching a glimpse of the dark interior.

Nilrem's ball was as big as a softball, but it was made of glass the color of clouds.

"What is that?" Jane asked.

Nilrem looked at her and blinked three times before answering. "Why, it is the ball," he told her as if he were saying the sky was blue, grass was green, and Ben was a pain in the neck.

"Ben would finally be able to shatter records if he used a bat on that," Annie said with a giggle.

"I believe bats prefer swooping across

the moon," Nilrem said, "unless the bats are different in Bailey City."

Kilmer patted his uncle's arm and nodded. "Everything is different in Bailey City," Kilmer said. "Once you get used to it I'm sure you'll want to stay a spell."

"Ah, yes," Nilrem said. "I haven't stayed a spell on a town for quite a while."

"You mean stay IN a town, don't you?" Annie asked.

Nilrem shook his head. "Of course not," he said matter-of-factly. "I've stayed spells in towns throughout all of time. Staying a spell ON a town is quite a different verse altogether."

This was sounding too much like English homework to Ben, and homework was the last thing he wanted to do. "Words, words, words," he said. "Daylight's wasting. Are we going to play softball or not?"

"Softball?" Nilrem asked. He tapped on the glass ball and sighed. "This is the only ball I have and it isn't soft at all. I didn't even know a softer version had been released. How can I ever keep up with the new technology?"

"No problem," Ben said. "We just need to trade your ball in for one of mine." Ben reached for the ball in Nilrem's hands, but Nilrem jerked the ball away before Ben could take it.

"Did you see that?" Jane whispered to Annie. "Ben did something to Nilrem's ball."

6

Useless

Ben's fingertips brushed against Nilrem's crystal ball. When they did, the white of the glass ball swirled like clouds during a spring storm. Annie was sure she saw the tiny figure of a person moving within it, but she couldn't be sure because Nilrem hid the ball within the folds of his robe.

"This ball has been in my possession for ages," Nilrem said with a sudden rumble to his voice. A frown creased his forehead, causing his bushy eyebrows to cast his eyes in dark shadows. "I am not ready to pass it on to another."

Ben only shrugged. "Your ball is useless here, anyway," he said.

Nilrem sighed. "I was afraid of that," he said sadly, the rumble suddenly gone from his voice. "It is the same wherever I go. My ways are no longer of any worth."

"Don't worry," Ben said. "I have everything we need. I'll be right back." Ben hurried to get his own softball and a bat while everyone else gathered at the dead end of Dedman Street.

"I'll show you how to play," Kilmer told his uncle. "It is very simple. All you have to do is swing a stick, hit Ben's ball, and then run to touch all the bases."

"First base is that oak tree," Jane pointed out.

"Second base is the garbage can," Annie said.

"And third base is the light pole," Kilmer told him.

"Ah, yes," Nilrem said. "I am familiar with the magic of threes."

"After you touch the light pole," Annie said, "you have to run back here to home plate."

"And then the magic happens?" Nilrem

asked. "Will there be lightning bolts and thunderclaps?"

"No," Annie said and giggled. "Only hand claps and cheering."

"Strange," Nilrem said. "But I shall give it a try."

Nilrem picked up the bat and held it in front of him like a knight holding a sword. Kilmer hurried to show him how to hold the bat over his shoulder. Then Ben wound up to pitch. The ball sped over home plate and Nilrem swung hard. But he missed, turning in a complete circle until stumbling to a dizzy stop.

"Strrriiike one!" Ben hollered.

"Keep your eyes on the ball," Jane told Nilrem.

Nilrem shook his head. "I prefer to keep them on my face," he said as Ben let loose another fastball. Nilrem barely had time to swing.

There was nothing Ben liked more than striking out a batter. "Strrriiike two!" he yelled with a grin.

Nilrem glared at Ben. "He is very irritating," Nilrem said.

Annie nodded. "Most people say that about Ben. Especially teachers. They say he gets the best of them."

"Well, he will not get the best of me," Nilrem said. He threw back his shoulders and held the bat straight above his head like the Statue of Liberty holding its torch. Then Nilrem spoke to the bat.

"Like the moon and the sun and the clouds in the sky, connect with that ball and send it up high!" When Nilrem finished speaking he used the bat to draw three invisible circles in the air. "We are ready," he finally said to Ben.

Ben grinned, wound up, and sent his famous curveball flying over home plate. Nobody ever hit Ben's curveballs. Nobody until Nilrem. The bat hit the ball with a deafening crack, sending it sailing so high in the sky the kids lost sight of it. They waited and waited and waited some more. But the ball never fell back to the ground.

"Wow," Annie said. "He hit that ball up high, just like he said he would in his funny rhyme."

Ben let out a low whistle. "I wish I could hit a ball like that," he said. "You make a great softball player!"

"That's not all he is, and that was no rhyme!" Jane said quietly. But her friends were so busy congratulating Nilrem, nobody heard her.

7
W-I-Z-A-R-D

Jane tugged on Annie's T-shirt to get her attention. "Don't you see what's happening?" she whispered to Annie. "Great-uncle Nilrem isn't an ordinary Hauntly relative."

"Of course not," Annie said. "All of Kilmer's relatives are strange. But he's very nice."

"He's more than nice," Jane told her. "He's a wizard!"

"He *is* very good at softball," Annie agreed. "But I wouldn't say he's a wizard at it."

"I meant a REAL wizard," Jane said. "One who casts spooky spells and tells the future using crystal balls."

Annie gasped. "You mean," she said, "that Nilrem's ball is a magical crystal ball?"

"Exactly," Jane said with a nod. "Remember how the colors swirled when Ben touched it. That can only mean one thing. It's full of magic."

"But," Annie said, "does that mean that Ben has magic, too? After all, it did react to his touch."

"If Ben is a wizard, then we're all in trouble," Jane said.

Annie and Jane looked at Ben. Ben had run home to grab another ball. Now he was getting ready to pitch it to Nilrem again. But Ben had to wait for Nilrem to finish talking to his bat first.

"Meteor, comet, flying star. Make Ben's softball travel far," Nilrem chanted.

When Ben pitched the ball, Nilrem's bat sent it flying over the Hauntlys' roof.

"Wow!" Ben yelled. Kilmer clapped. Annie cheered. But Jane crossed her arms over her chest and glared at Nilrem.

"Too bad we can't play anymore," Ben said. "I'm out of softballs!"

"I was just getting the hang of this

31

game," Nilrem said sadly. "That's the way it always is. I get used to things one way, and then they change."

"Don't worry, Great-uncle Nilrem," Kilmer told his uncle as they headed back down Dedman Street toward Hauntly Manor Inn. "There are many interesting things in Bailey City. You won't get bored!"

Ben collected his bat and joined Annie and Jane clustered near third base. "Nilrem sure can hit a ball," Ben said. "Maybe he can teach me how to make a ball disappear into thin air!"

"Don't even mention that," Jane blurted. "Or we could be in big trouble."

"What are you huffing about?" Ben asked. "You act like you just saw a genie fly by on a magic carpet."

"I didn't see a genie," Jane said, "but you are right about one thing. I am talking about magic."

Annie nodded. "Jane thinks the only way Nilrem could hit balls so far is by casting magic spells."

Ben laughed so hard he had to sit on the sidewalk. "That spelling bee has put spells on your brain," he said, "and in your imagination."

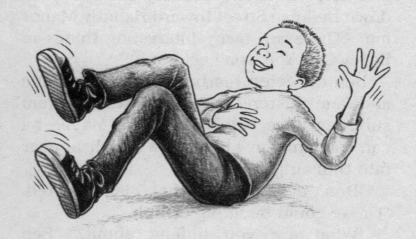

"I'll spell something for you," Jane said and poked Ben on his head. "W-I-Z-A-R-D! Wizard. And that's exactly what Great-uncle Nilrem is!"

8

Merlin

"You really believe Kilmer's uncle Nilrem is a wizard?" Ben asked between giggles.

"Stranger things have happened at the Hauntlys'," Annie pointed out. "Maybe we should listen to Jane."

"Even if he is a wizard, what difference does it make?" Ben asked. "He's a nice guy. We don't have to worry."

"Of course we have to worry," Jane said. "If somebody like Issy finds out Uncle Nilrem is a wizard, there could be BIG trouble. And I mean B-I-G," Jane said, spelling the word to make sure Ben understood.

Ben slapped himself on the forehead and jumped up from the sidewalk. "You're right!" he shouted.

"I am?" Jane asked. She wasn't used to Ben agreeing with her.

35

Ben nodded. "If Uncle Nilrem is a wizard, then we HAVE to keep it a secret in order to win."

"Win what?" Annie asked.

"The spelling bee!" Ben said as if he'd just discovered a way to fly to Pluto. "If you're right and Uncle Nilrem is a wizard, then he can cast a magic spell on us. A spelling spell!"

Annie shook her finger in front of her brother's nose. "That's cheating," she told him. "We have to play fair."

"Playing fair means I'd have to study," Ben said. "I may believe in wizards, but I definitely don't believe in studying!"

"Well, I believe in studying," Annie said. "So does Kilmer. I'm not going to stand here and listen to you make plans to cheat. I'm going to go study with Kilmer."

Annie marched down the sidewalk without looking back at her friends a single time.

"Do you really believe Nilrem is a wizard?" Ben asked Jane.

Jane nodded. "There's only one kind of

person who travels with his own crystal ball," Jane pointed out. "And that's a wizard."

"Wizards only lived in olden times," Ben told her. "And they were named Merlin."

Jane hit her forehead with the palm of her hand. "Of course," she said. "You're absolutely right."

Ben stood up straight and grinned. "So you don't believe Nilrem is a wizard anymore?"

Jane shook her head. "I believe it even more," she said. "Look."

Jane bent down and used her finger to write N-I-L-R-E-M in the dirt. "Don't you see it?" Jane asked.

"I see you're too busy spelling words to make sense," Ben told her.

"Look again," Jane said. This time she started at the end of the word. "Nilrem spelled backwards is Merlin! This proves that Kilmer's great-uncle is a wizard!"

"I know one way to find out for sure," Ben said.

"You're not planning to take his crystal ball, are you?" Jane asked.

"You always think of the hard way to get information," Ben said. "All we have to do is ask him!"

Without waiting for Jane, Ben headed straight for Uncle Nilrem's mobile home. He pounded on the back door three times before it slowly swung open. Nilrem peered down at the two kids and waited for them to speak.

"We thought you might like some company," Ben said.

Nilrem nodded and held open the door for Ben and Jane. Slowly, they climbed the three steps into the van. They blinked, waiting for their eyes to get used to the dark interior.

There wasn't much inside Nilrem's van. A table with two chairs sat in the far corner. The cloudy ball was perched on a little stand in the center of the table. A cot lined another wall, and it was covered by a quilt stitched with bright yellow stars. But Ben

didn't notice any of that. He was staring straight up. Tiny glow-in-the-dark stars were plastered all over the ceiling.

"Wow," Ben said. "I wish my bedroom had a ceiling like this."

Nilrem smiled. "I am sure I can arrange to make your wish come true," he said. "Since the beginning of time I have fallen asleep with the stars watching me from above. I follow them on my travels by day and they guide my dream trips at night."

"You make it sound like you've been alive forever," Jane said. "How can that be?"

Nilrem smiled and pointed to the chairs by the table. Jane and Ben sat down and Nilrem settled himself on the floor.

"I have traveled far during my long life. I've seen the sun rise over deserts and mountains, fields and oceans. I've consulted with kings and queens and sultans."

"You must be a very important person," Ben said.

Nilrem sighed. "Perhaps in my younger days I was," he said. "But now my beard is long and white. No one sees the use of my old ways. I was hoping things would be different here in Bailey City," he said. "But I am afraid I was mistaken. There is no place left on Earth for me. No place."

Nilrem looked so sad sitting on the floor of his motor home that Jane couldn't keep her mouth shut.

"Bailey City is different," she said. "You'll see!"

9
Spelling Spell

"Why did you tell Great-uncle Nilrem that Bailey City is different?" Ben asked. He and Jane had just left the motor home and were heading for Hauntly Manor Inn. They could see Kilmer and Annie sitting on the front steps.

Jane shrugged. "I was just trying to cheer him up. He seemed so sad."

"I guess it's hard getting old," Ben agreed.

"What's hard is not feeling wanted," Jane pointed out as they stepped on the broken sidewalk in front of Hauntly Manor Inn. "We have to find a way to make him feel useful."

Kilmer looked at his spelling list and said, "Receive."

Annie scratched her head and started

spelling the word slowly. "R . . . e . . . c . . . i," she began.

"Wrong!" Ben shouted. "Even I know that word."

Annie frowned at Ben. "It's no use," she said sadly. "I'll never learn these words in time for the spelling bee."

Nilrem suddenly appeared behind Ben and Annie. He had a big smile on his face. "I know how to help you," he said.

"No," Jane said quickly, but it was too late.

Nilrem had already started his rhyme, "Annie shall spell every letter. No one here will do it better!"

"Hey," Issy yelled from the sidewalk in front of Kilmer's house. "What kind of weird stuff are you doing up there?"

"Oh, no," Jane moaned. "Now what are we going to do?"

Nilrem rubbed his long beard. "Have I done something wrong?" he asked.

Jane patted Nilrem on the shoulder.

"Everything's fine," she said. "We just have to talk to Issy."

"What about the spell?" Annie asked.

"We'll worry about that later," Ben said, running down the sidewalk toward Issy.

"Hi, Issy," Jane said. "I guess you heard us kidding around."

Issy put her hands on her hips. "It didn't sound like that old man was kidding to me. He sounded very serious. As a matter of fact, he sounded like some kind of wizard chanting spooky spells."

Annie laughed as she came up beside Ben. "Don't be silly," Annie told Issy.

"I'm not being silly. I'm worried," Issy said. "I'm worried about the safety of Bailey City with that strange man around. I have half a mind to go to the police."

Ben laughed. "You're right about one thing. You only have half a mind."

"That's it!" Issy snapped. "I'm going to the police right after school tomorrow. Then we'll see who'll be laughing!"

10
Winner

"This is horrible," Annie said the next day after school.

"Winning the third-grade spelling bee is horrible?" Jane asked. "It sounds pretty good to me."

The kids were gathered around Annie. She had surprised everybody by winning the third-grade spelling bee. No matter what the words were, Annie seemed to know them all.

Annie shook her head. "It's not fair. Howie Jones should have won. He's the smartest kid in our grade. He would have won if it hadn't been for Uncle Nilrem's magic spell. Now he's just the runner-up."

"But being a runner-up is just as good," Jane pointed out. "Runner-ups get to be in tomorrow's schoolwide spelling bee, too. Howie could win then."

Ben swung his backpack on his back and frowned at Annie. "You would complain about winning a million dollars. You don't know for sure that Uncle Nilrem is a wizard, but even if he did cast a spelling spell, it was a favor. But all you do is whine."

Annie shrugged. "I know he meant well, but I don't want to win unfairly. I'm not a cheater. We have to get Uncle Nilrem to un-spell the spell."

"Can wizards do that?" Jane asked.

"I guess so," Annie said. "Maybe he can say the rhyme backward or something."

"If you ask him to take his spell back, you might hurt his feelings," Ben pointed out.

"That's true," Jane admitted. "He seemed so sad yesterday. We can't make it worse by hurting his feelings."

Ben nodded. "If he thinks he did something wrong, he won't feel useful."

"I want Uncle Nilrem to be happy," Annie said, "but I also want to be fair. Now I don't know what to do."

"Well, I know what to do," Ben said. "I want to play softball, and there's Kilmer."

"We can't," Jane said, "unless you found your softballs."

"Besides," Annie said, "Kilmer said he would help me study for tomorrow's schoolwide spelling bee."

"How can you study on a beautiful day like this?" Ben asked.

"Easy," Annie said. "I want to win that spelling bee, fair and square. That means I have to study." Annie hurried to walk home with Kilmer. Ben could hear his sister and Kilmer practicing spelling words as they walked.

Ben rolled his eyes. "This spelling bee is really starting to bug me."

"The spelling contest is the least of our troubles," Jane said. "If Uncle Nilrem really is a wizard who thinks he's useless, there's no telling what he might try."

"You're getting your pigtails tied in a knot over nothing," Ben told her. "Uncle Nilrem seems harmless to me."

"Oh, yeah?" Jane asked. "What if he decides to help teachers instead of kids? He could help them whip up homework, tests, and other horrible tortures."

"That would be terrible," Ben said. Suddenly a big smile spread across Ben's face. "But don't worry, I have a brilliant idea."

"What is it?" Jane asked.

"I'm not telling," Ben said. "You'll just have to wait until tomorrow morning. And then you'll see just how brilliant I really am."

11

Old-fashioned Spelling

"This is it?" Jane asked Ben the next morning. "Your brilliant plan?"

Annie, Jane, and Ben were waiting for Kilmer on the Hauntlys' front porch. Ben had just finished telling Jane how he was going to save the day.

"Let's count all your ideas," Ben told Jane and acted as if he were adding numbers in the air. "I've got the answer. It's a big fat Z-E-R-O!"

Jane curled her fingers into a fist and held it in front of Ben's nose. "I'll make you a deal," she said. "If you never come up with any more ideas, I won't punch you in the nose for an entire day!"

Annie put her hand on Jane's arm. "Ben's plan might actually work," she said. "Lots of kids at Bailey School need extra

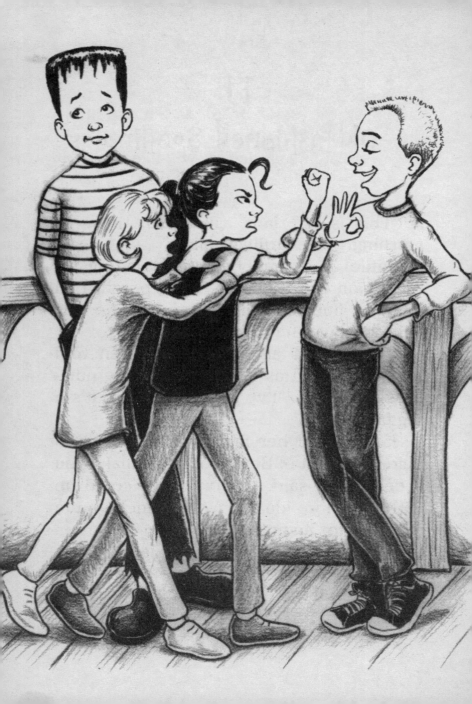

help, especially in spelling. Kilmer's great-uncle Nilrem says he's good at spelling. Maybe if he helps the kids at school, he'll feel useful again. Teachers will like it, too. It may be the perfect plan."

"It's true Uncle Nilrem may be good at spelling," Jane said, "but what kind of spelling? What if he uses his spooky spells to turn all the teachers into wizards?"

"I wouldn't like that," Ben admitted. "I think he should teach me how to be a wizard instead. He could show me how to turn teachers into frogs, principals into newts, and homework into puffs of smoke."

"He's not teaching anybody how to make magic spells," Annie said. "I talked to him last night. The only spelling Uncle Nilrem agreed to do is with letters. L-E-T-T-E-R-S! I asked him to take the spelling spell off me, too."

Ben was ready to argue, but just then the heavy wooden door of Hauntly Manor Inn finally creaked open. Boris stuck his head out and smiled down at the three kids. Annie noticed his pointy eyeteeth looked whiter than usual.

"Hilda and I have finished," Boris said, swinging open the door.

Jane gasped. Ben gulped. But Annie smiled. "You look wonderful!" she said.

Kilmer and Hilda gave Nilrem a little shove from behind and he stepped onto the porch. Nilrem's beard was completely gone and his hair had been cut up over his ears. He looked like a stranger to the kids, but they recognized Nilrem as soon as he bowed.

"Do you really like the new me?" Nilrem asked.

Ben patted Nilrem's back. "Of course," Ben said. "That long hair and beard made you look a thousand years old. It's time you changed with the times!"

Hilda brushed loose hairs from Nilrem's shoulder. "Ben is correct," she said softly. "Things never stay the same. Why should we?"

"Perhaps you are right," Nilrem said.

"Now I just hope I can make a little modern-day magic at school today!"

"There's only one way to find out," Kilmer said, stepping onto the porch. "And that's by trying!"

The four kids led Kilmer's great-uncle Nilrem to Bailey Elementary. As soon as they reached the school, Jane pulled Annie aside. "You have to keep your eyes on Uncle Nilrem," she said. "Make sure he doesn't slip in a few spooky spells."

"We've already gone over that," Annie said. "Uncle Nilrem agreed to use old-fashioned spelling."

"Old-fashioned spelling," Jane said, "is exactly what I'm afraid of!"

Annie hurried to catch up with Nilrem. She introduced him to all the teachers at Bailey Elementary. Mrs. Jeepers, a third-grade teacher, smiled an odd little half-smile when she met Nilrem. Mrs. Jeepers was from Transylvania and most kids thought she was a vampire. Annie hid behind Nilrem when he shook Mrs. Jeepers' hand. Annie figured a wizard was good protection against vampires.

All day long, Nilrem sat at the back of Annie's classroom, helping kids from the third grade with their spelling words. Annie listened closely. She didn't hear a single rhyme.

Nilrem helped a third-grader named Carey. "Enchanting," Nilrem said.

Carey batted her eyelashes. "That's the perfect word for me," she said. Carey's father was the president of Bailey City Bank and she pretended she was the most popular girl in the universe. "E-N-C-H-A-N-T-I-N-G. Enchanting."

Nilrem smiled. Next he helped a chubby boy named Huey. "Potion," Nilrem said.

Huey grinned. "That's easy," he said. "P-O-T-I-O-N. Potion."

"Wonderful," Nilrem told him.

Annie smiled to herself. Everything was going according to plan. Nilrem was helping the kids study spelling the old-fashioned way. The kids were getting better at spelling, and Nilrem was happy to be helping.

Howie Jones came in next. Nilrem gave him hard words like *bewitching* and *mesmerizing,* but Howie got every one correct.

After Howie, Nilrem sent for the fourth-graders. Issy pranced into the third-grade class. She stopped by Annie's desk. "This isn't going to work," Issy whispered to Annie. "I'm calling the police right after school and telling them all about your plans to win the spelling bee. Kilmer and his batty relatives aren't getting away with planting a wizard right here in Bailey Elementary!"

Annie ignored Issy, but she did scoot her desk closer to hear what Nilrem and Issy said.

Nilrem smiled at Issy when she sat down at the table. Issy didn't smile back. She crossed her arms over her chest and frowned.

"Are you ready to study spelling?" Nilrem asked. "Spell *incantation.*"

Issy shook her head. "I don't believe in spelling your magical words," she said. "And neither does Bailey City. I'm going to make sure your spelling ways disappear forever!"

Annie groaned. Issy was being ruder than usual.

Nilrem didn't disappear, but he did frown. When he spoke, Annie heard the unhappy rumble in his voice. She gasped when she recognized something else, too. A rhyme.

"I've played your spelling game fair and square. But all you have done is stare and glare," Nilrem said to Issy. "My own style of spelling is needed here, to make your sneers simply disappear!"

And then Nilrem snapped his fingers once, twice, three times right in front of Issy's eyes.

12
Dizzy Issy

"There's something wrong with Issy," Jane whispered.

"I've known that all along," Ben said.

"No," Jane said, "I mean REALLY wrong."

Jane and Ben sat on the floor in the Bailey School gymnasium. The spelling bee was ready to begin. Annie sat on a folding chair on the stage along with Issy, Howie, and the other runner-ups. Annie and most of the other kids were concentrating on remembering their spelling words. Not Issy. Issy looked out at the audience. She giggled, she laughed, and then Issy giggled some more.

"I don't think I've ever seen Issy laugh like that," Ben said. "Somebody must've tickled her funny bone."

Jane shook her head. "It's worse than

61

that. Remember the rhyme Annie over-
heard Uncle Nilrem say? I think that rhyme
was a spell to cheer up Issy. Only his spell
was too strong."

"Then we should be thanking him for
turning Mean Issy into Dizzy Issy," Ben said
with a laugh.

Jane wasn't sure Ben was right, but there
was nothing she could do about it because
just then Kilmer scooted into the empty
space next to her. He pointed to the back of
the room. "My whole family came to see this
exciting contest of spelling," Kilmer said.

Jane and Ben spotted Hilda and Boris
sitting in the back of the auditorium. Nilrem
sat between them. All three smiled and
waved at the kids.

Jane waved back, then glanced at the
rest of the grown-ups in the audience.
When she did, she spotted something by
the door that made her groan.

"What's the matter?" Ben asked.

"Issy really did it," she told him. "She
called the police!"

Sure enough, two officers dressed in blue stood at the doors. They were busy staring into the crowd. Jane knew exactly who they were looking for. Uncle Nilrem.

"We have to do something," Kilmer said. "There's no telling what will happen if they find Uncle Nilrem."

But the kids didn't get a chance because just then Principal Davis climbed the steps to the stage. Principal Davis wiped his bald head with a handkerchief before speaking.

When he did, Issy broke into another fit of giggles. Principal Davis glared at her, but that just made Issy laugh harder.

"Welcome to the final round of the Bailey Elementary Spelling Bee," he said. "These finalists have studied and practiced for weeks. Today we will see who will be the Spelling Bee champion!"

The audience clapped, Ben cheered, but Issy just sat on the stage and laughed.

One after the other, the kids on the stage took their place in front of the microphone while Principal Davis drew words from a fishbowl for them to spell. And one after the other, the kids did their best. Unfortunately, sometimes their best wasn't enough. Carey missed a letter in *mysterious*. Huey spelled *rhyme* with an *i* instead of a *y*.

Every time somebody made a mistake, Issy held her stomach and laughed. Of course, Issy laughed when a contestant spelled a word correctly, too. Issy even laughed when she was spelling a word herself. In fact, Issy laughed so much, people in the audience got tickled, too. Soon everybody was smiling or giggling. Even the two police officers near the door couldn't help laughing.

"This is terrible," Jane said between giggles. "Uncle Nilrem's cheerful spell has infected the entire audience."

Ben held his stomach. "At least our teachers can't yell at us," he snorted. "They're too busy laughing!"

That just made Jane double over. But the spelling bee continued, and finally there were only three spellers left: Annie, Howie, and Issy. Principal Davis mopped off his head and peered at the contestants. His stomach looked as if it were full of jumping beans when he tried to hold in his laughter. "The next word," he said, "is for Howie. The word is *incantation*."

Howie thought before he spelled. But, unfortunately, he didn't get it right.

Principal Davis shook his head. "I'm sorry," he said. "The word goes to Issy." Issy hopped up to the microphone.

Annie recognized the word *incantation*. It was the same one Nilrem tried to help Issy with the day before. Issy should have let him help her, because when she tried to spell it, Issy forgot two letters.

Principal Davis shook his head and looked at Annie. Annie took her place at the microphone. She spoke loudly and clearly. "I-N-C-A-N-T-A-T-I-O-N. Incantation."

"Correct!" Principal Davis bellowed. "We have a winner!"

Issy grabbed the microphone and screamed, "STOP! There is a cheating spell in this room!"

Principal Davis held his stomach and laughed. "Don't you mean a spelling cheater?" he asked when he finally caught his breath.

The entire audience howled with laughter.

Principal Davis took back the microphone. "This spelling bee has been fun, but we must remember it is an important occasion. It is no joking matter."

Issy stood in the middle of the stage and turned red. "I'm not telling a joke," Issy said. "Just ask Annie. The Hauntlys and their uncle Nilrem have made this spelling bee a howling disaster by helping Annie cheat with a magic spelling spell."

All eyes turned to the Hauntlys sitting in the back row of the auditorium. The police officers weren't laughing anymore. They headed straight for Uncle Nilrem. Annie had to do something. Fast.

She grabbed the microphone from Principal Davis. "Issy is right!" Annie said, her words booming across the gymnasium.

"Oh, no," Jane groaned. "What has Annie done?"

13
The Most Powerful Magic of All

The audience froze. Nobody said a word.

"Uncle Nilrem worked a powerful spell on all of us," she said. "He used the most powerful magic of all."

Ben groaned. Jane gasped. Kilmer moaned. But Annie didn't notice. She kept right on talking.

"Uncle Nilrem helped us study. He played softball with us. He told us about when he was young. In other words, he was our friend. And that is the most powerful magic of all!"

The audience clapped. Boris and Hilda cheered. Nilrem bowed. Everybody stood to give him a standing ovation.

Principal Davis took back the microphone from Annie and spoke above all the

cheering. "We have two winners today," he said. "Annie and Uncle Nilrem!"

Everybody was so busy clapping for Nilrem, they didn't notice when Issy marched off the stage and out of the gymnasium.

The next day Annie, Ben, and Jane knocked on the door to Hauntly Manor Inn. Kilmer opened the door and greeted his friends.

"Uncle Nilrem's mobile home is gone," Ben said sadly. "Has he left for good?"

"Don't worry about Great-uncle Nilrem," Kilmer said with a smile. "Thanks to Annie, my uncle is happy. He decided schools are magical places to be. He left early this morning to begin studying!"

"Studying!" Ben gasped. "Why would your uncle need to study?"

"To become a teacher," Kilmer said.

Issy walked by just in time to hear Kilmer. "I'm glad he's gone!" she said. "Your uncle made me the laughingstock of Bailey

Elementary School. I'll get even with him for that if he ever shows his face in Bailey City again!"

"You didn't need help from anybody," Ben pointed out. "You made a laughingstock of yourself all on your own!"

Issy shook a fist at Ben. "You'll be sorry you ever said that," she said before stomping down Dedman Street.

"I wonder what happened to Uncle Nilrem's cheerful spell on Issy," Jane said.

"We don't know for sure that Uncle Nilrem even cast a wizard's spell on her," Annie said.

"Then why did Issy turn the spelling bee into a gigglefest?" Ben asked.

"Maybe she was just nervous," Annie said. "A lot of people get the giggles when they're in front of big groups of people."

"There's one thing we do know for sure," Jane said with a sigh. "Things are back to normal on Dedman Street."

"As if anything is ever N-O-R-M-A-L on Dedman Street!" Annie said.

About the Authors

Marcia Thornton Jones and Debbie Dadey like to write about monsters. Their first series with Scholastic, **The Adventures of the Bailey School Kids,** has many characters who are *monsterously* funny. Now with the Hauntly family, Marcia and Debbie are in monster heaven!

Marcia and Debbie both used to live in Lexington, Kentucky. They were teachers at the same elementary school. When Debbie moved to Aurora, Illinois, she and Marcia had to change how they worked together. These authors now create monster books long-distance. They play hot potato with their stories, passing them back and forth by computer.

About the Illustrator

John Steven Gurney is the illustrator of both **The Bailey City Monsters** and **The Adventures of the Bailey School Kids.** He uses real people in his own neighborhood as models when he draws the characters in Bailey City. John has illustrated many books for young readers. He lives in Vermont with his wife and two children.

The Adventures of THE BAILEY SCHOOL KIDS

by Debbie Dadey and
Marcia Thornton Jones

Blast Off With The Bailey School Kids!

It's an out-of-this-world adventure!
The Bailey School Kids are going to
space camp. They'll get to train for
space missions like real astronauts
for a whole week. There's only one
problem: Their vampire teacher is
coming along for the ride!

Look for The Bailey School Kids
Super Special #4:

Mrs. Jeepers in Outer Space

Coming in June